HEY BO

A BOTTLE WHO LEARNED TO APPRECIATE THE PRESENT

ADITI ARYA

Made with ♥ on the Notion Press Platform
www.notionpress.com

This book is dedicated to you,
keep working hard and one day
you will live the life you
imagined for yourself

Contents

About The Author

Aditi Arya the author of this motivational fiction book is a very ambitious and hard working girl. She never gets afraid from setbacks and she keeps going in every situation of her life. Currently she is investing her time for her dream project and she is looking forward to become an successful author. This is her second book, she has already published her first book titled as "The Secrets UNLOCKED"

Preface

An expensive water bottle named BO was picked up from a supermarket by a businessman. BO had a lot of expectations about life outside the supermarket. For him a life of an expensive water bottle meant popularity and rich lifestyle but when he saw what real world looks like, his whole ego went to zero and he learned 18 valuable life lessons throughout his journey.

This is a short story but its a very valuable journey. When you will turn the pages you will know what kind of lesson make a person a better human being.

PREFACE

An expensive water bottle named BO was picked up from a supermarket by a businessman. BO had a lot of expectations about life outside the supermarket. For him a life of an expensive water bottle meant popularity and a [illegible] lifestyle but when he [illegible] real world in his life, [illegible] he learned valuable life lessons throughout his journey.

This is a short story but its a very valuable journey. When you will turn the pages you will know what kind of lesson make a person a better human being.

I

Journey Starts from Here

Good morning, I can see some beautiful rays of sunlight, making this supermarket alive, coming straight from the entrance. Before getting started with this amazing valuable story, let me introduce myself. I am Aly, the voice of this story or simply you can say that I am the anchor of this story. I will be taking you to a very powerful journey of a Water Bottle named BO. He is not an ordinary water bottle; rather he is an "expensive" one. However, throughout his journey he learned being expensive is good, but if we are able to add value in someone's life, that is a level up feeling. His life is full of surprises and adventures. He has learned some of the most important life lessons everyone should learn and use in their life.

Before starting the story, let us wake up our sweet little BO! BO is the expensive water bottle (in terms of price) in this supermarket named Express Mart. He has been here for 3 days now and he is keenly waiting to be purchased one day, so that he can travel this beautiful world. I think today is his day of getting purchased, you know my gut feeling says that let's see what happens.

I greeted BO with a smile; Hi BO! It's time to wake up!

BO replied while yawning; Good Morning Aly!

See BO who all are here today to see you; I said.

Oh! Hi you beautiful people. My name is BO! I am a water bottle, no no... Not a simple one but an expensive water bottle that carries the healthiest water; BO said with excitement.

Hey BO, I have already introduced who you are. By the way, did you sleep well last night? I asked.

Yes, Aly pretty well! But hey Aly, let them guess what water I carry inside me; BO replied. Have a quick guess, till then let me enjoy the cold wind that's coming from the AC of this supermarket. Ahh! Cool, just like me. By the way, in this supermarket, I am the most expensive water bottle ever kept, but the only issue I face is they do not respect me, you know. The way I should be treated is missing somehow, but never mind, it is a nice place to be; BO added.

Hey BO! respect what you have. They treat you really well by the way. I replied.

Before going further, did you guess what water he carries? Here is the hint, you mostly see his friends in paparazzi clicking their pictures with celebrities; I said.

Come on, now it is simple to answer, I am an alkaline water bottle, the best choice for health freak people and celebs for sure. Yes! The rich people love me to drink and keep me with them, and why not I am expensive plus healthy to drink and keep; BO added.

BO never knew what real world looks like. He has mostly seen his friends with celebs and health freaks, and he assumes that whatever he sees on the television is "perfect" and life out there is wonderful. But the reality is always surreptitious to every story. We are shown what is perfect to display in front of us, but we never get the opportunity to see and feel the reality of everything. The real world is way more different from what BO! thinks about all the time. He has made the images "too perfect" but in reality, we can only make things close to perfect. Everyone or everything is not perfect, we make some of our things close to perfect but not totally perfect.

Hey you Aly, let me ask you a question; Have you ever seen an ordinary bottle with the riches? No! Along with me, they love my friends who have become a celeb now and, soon I will become one. You just keep watching Aly! You have never seen my friends without paparazzi or a celeb. In addition, if they deserve this, I deserve better always! And if you think that other bottles are superior than me, you will see one day, I will rule the world of bottles; BO added in arrogance

Hi BO! Someone greeted from behind.

Wait who is that, BO said.

I am Roz, a very calm and sweet rose water drink, she replied. You look so handsome BO, I have heard a lot about you and I am happy to see you in person, she said with a smile on her face.

Oh! Hi Roz, aaa...thanks for the complement. By the way where did you hear about me? BO asked with a shy face.

Oh, I heard about you at the last place I was kept, and I was shifted here last night only. The other bottles said that you are the only expensive bottle here, is that true BO. Roz asked.

Ahh, yes, I am the expensive plus the healthiest bottle of water here, BO said with confidence.

Ohm, so great to hear that, Roz replied.

See, Aly! Bottles know me, they listen to me and respect me. And if I have a bit of ego, that's ok because that is what makes me Expensive water container; BO said.

BO didn't know what was going to happen the next moment. But always remember, ego is what destroys everything weather good or bad.

BO and Roz were having a very nice and sweet conversation. Roz is a rose flavoured juice that is popular over here. Whenever it's time to drink something refreshing, it's always Roz. When BO and Roz were having the conversation, a customer entered the supermarket. He was the first customer of the day. He was looking like a businessman and a pretty rich person. Oh, wait he is moving towards BO! Is he going to buy BO now? I think so...

Oh, a customer coming towards me. Ooo, expensive watch, phone and expensive fragrance. Will he buy me? Ohh, damn yes, he picked me up! BO said in excitement.

Ah, I think you are sold already BO, Roz said.

Oh, yes Roz I am always sold to the riches, BO said with excitement. Ahh finally going out of this old supermarket where I didn't deserve to be. Now, I will become the celeb overnight, lots of paparazzi and most importantly my swag!

BO's new and adventurous journey started the next moment he stepped out of that supermarket. He thought it was great to be around the riches but it's never what you think it should be. Life is all about surprises and many lessons.

WHAT!!!! An expensive car, I am going in this beauty now. Straight from supermarket to the place I deserved. Let us goooo!!! BO said with excitement.

Hey you Aly, you called me what, egoistic, see where I am right now! keep looking at my success and see where I am sitting right now! A dam big expensive car that will take me to my new home. BO added.

The customer who bought BO was a businessman who lived in a luxury apartment near the seas. He was a busy man yet a bit selfish, I can say. He only cares about him and his work for sure and when you are with a man like him, you never know where an empty bottle will go. But the materialistic luxuries made BO so blind that he didn't even see what was coming on his way. What we can say, Best of Luck BO!

The car trip from the supermarket to the luxury apartment was 45 minutes long and, in this stretch, BO enjoyed the car ride pretty well. He was kept in the front bottle holder near the hand gear and from there he was having the full view of that open sunroof car. He could see the blue sky with the views of sky-high buildings and beautiful nature. He was so amazed by the beauty that for first 10 minutes, his mouth was wide open and his eyes were popping out. For him, it was something he imagined from the very beginning. The buildings were reflecting in his eyes and his whole body was expecting that he is finally living the life he imagined.

Ahh, reached home after an amazing and magical ride. Hey Aly, the ride was magical and unforgettable. Seriously, Aly I am enjoying my new life, BO said while the businessman was parking his car.

I am happy for you BO! You are into something you imagined, enjoy your best times BO. I said.

BO and that businessman were going towards the apartment from the parking area. BO was looking at the building with amaze and seriously the building was 18 storeys tall and the businessman lived on the top floor. They entered the building and took the lift. It was BO's first lift ride and he got scared, but somehow managed his emotions and tried to enjoy the lift ride. After few minutes they reached the top floor. The moment that businessman opened the door, BO couldn't control his excitement. The apartment was nothing but looked like a crystal palace with a beautiful view of that amazing city. The businessman slowly started to go towards his lavish big balcony. The moment BO entered the balcony, he saw the most beautiful view ever seen. We can imagine the view of a city from 18th floor!

The businessman kept BO on the table and sat next to him in the chair. BO was continuously looking at the mesmerizing view from the balcony. The cold breeze was touching BO's cheeks, there was complete silence, only the chirping of birds and the cool fresh air. BO was completely into the moment; he didn't even realise that the businessman took some sips from BO.

Hey Aly, look at this magical view. I can't even describe it in words! BO said while feeling the breezy air.

Yes, BO you are right, the view is amazing. I can feel your excitement and happiness you are experiencing now. I said.

Aly, I want to live like this forever! I want to be here as long as this cold breeze says bye to me. BO said with tears in his eyes.

BO! you should focus on today, the now you are in. We don't have the control on our future but we can control our feelings between different situations. I said.

I know Aly, but we should also take care about our future. BO replied.

I do not mean to say that. It is not bad to imagine the future but I meant to say that first enjoy what you have now and then let the today decide your tomorrow. I replied.

Ok Aly as you say so, BO answered while enjoying the view.

Time passed by and BO was sitting on the table where the businessman was working on the other side on his laptop. After a while, the businessman took BO from the balcony and stored him in the fridge.

In the fridge, BO met other bottles also. He saw many expensive bottles of juices, sauces, drinks etc. chilling there and enjoying the cold breeze cooling the fridge. The moment BO entered the fridge, every bottle looked at BO for few seconds and then they got busy with their jobs. It seemed like the other bottles did not even care that they have a new member among themselves. Nevertheless, ignoring what just happened, BO gathered some courage and greeted every bottle with a smile on his face.

Hi bottles, myself BO! BO greeted in joy.

Hi BO! it's so good to see you; one of the bottles replied.

We can be friends, right? BO asked.

Friends!? For how long? Few hours; one of the bottles replied.

F..ew hours? BO asked in a confused tonality.

Yes, few hours because you are a water container, he will drink you and leave you for recycling; said Sid, one among those bottles.

REALLY!!!! He will not reuse me? He will leave me to recycle so soon? BO asked in shock.

Yes BO! But don't worry, you will become another nice bottle after recycling; said Sid.

But I don't want be recycled so soon! I want to enjoy more. And I am expensive so I don't think he will recycle me so soon; he will carry me with him; BO replied.

BO! we have seen a lot of bottles like you, they come today and go tomorrow; Replied Sid.

This sentence made BO a little scared and sad. He thought he can stay here for long and enjoy some luxury stuffs but it was not possible here. First time in his life he started to feel himself worthless and useless.

Lesson #1

Nothing remains with us forever, if today we have something, tomorrow we will have something completely different from the last one.

Life always finds its way to teach us lessons that are worth taking. And always be prepared for surprises that will make you be prepared for any situation and will help you become emotionally strong.

He stayed in the fridge for the whole night. He was looking at all the bottles enjoying their company but BO; he was sitting in the corner with a half-empty juice can. Later in the morning, the businessman took BO from the fridge and kept him in the counter top of the kitchen. It seemed like the businessman was going somewhere.

Hey Aly, the businessman is talking about some meeting that is going to happen today morning. I think he is taking me there! BO said.

Hmm, I also think the same BO! be ready for another road trip. I replied.

Yes Aly, I am born ready for road trips and some paparazzi! I think the paparazzi will finally see one more expensive bottle with an expensive man. BO said in excitement.

I appreciate BO! that you are an expensive bottle of water but you should be prepared for every situation, I said.

I am already prepared Aly, I will find some paparazzi, I will sit in an expensive meeting with tons of gentleman talking about business and market. And after the meeting, I will come back in the fridge and will say Hi!!! to that bottle Sid, whose non-sense made my entire night a night mare. BO said.

The road trip began in the expensive car! BO was kept in the bottle holder in front and the businessman was driving the car. BO was somehow enjoying the trip and the sceneries, but he was bit scared by the last night comments of that bottle Sid. The road trip was about 2.5 hours long and by the time they were about to reach, the businessman took another sip from BO, but this time big ones. BO was already half empty and nervous too.

Hey Aly, I am not half empty, I am half full. Stop calling me empty! This businessman seemed to be a nice guy; he will definitely reuse me to keep water cool in his refrigerator. And for sure, I will meet that bottle whatever his name was and will teach him a good lesson. BO said.

The businessman parked the car in the parking lot. From BO's point of view, he was supposed to take BO with him for the meeting but the opposite happened. He was left alone in the car yes; the businessman did not take BO with him for the meeting. Rather he left BO is the car all by himself. BO was really angry and sad, he thought he was supposed to be the part of that meeting but he was left behind.

It was just the beginning for BO, there was more to come his way. BO was sitting in the bottle holder, looking for the businessman with a hope that when he would feel thirsty, he would pick up BO from here. But the wait was way too long. BO started to feel exhausted and very dull, he was losing all hopes. For him, being an expensive water bottle meant paparazzi and celebs, but the reality was very much different than he thought. I really feel bad for BO.

Lesson #2

What we see from inside is not always the reality of any situation, there is a big difference between reality and what is shown upfront. To know the reality of the situation, we have to step outside, we have to accept the truth completely, we have to see the things as it is and then, we have to change our thought process accordingly. When you accept any situation as it is, suddenly you will see yourself enjoying it.

BO only saw what was shown upfront, he didn't know the reality of life and the challenges we all face in our life. Life is way more different than we think life should be. Life is not always in our favour and if you want life to be in your favour, work for it and

make it happen.

Hey Aly, how long I have to wait for that businessman, it's already been 2 hours now. I am losing all hopes for a good and expensive life, not expensive any more but good life at least. BO said in a sad tonality.

Hey BO! Don't worry, you will be fine and here is a very important moral; never put too must trust behind someone because people change in no time. I replied.

Ok Aly, I understand.... wait Hey, I can see the businessman, he is coming with some other people. Let me see if he wants me to be with him. BO said in excitement.

BO! saw the businessman coming towards the car with his few colleagues. The reason he was returning to the car was that he left behind some documents. He was coming to take those documents not BO! But BO was thinking that he was coming to take BO with him. BO made the same mistake again; he again placed too much trust on and he did not take BO this time as well.

BO started to cry and of course! got angrier than before. BO was only looking outside the car window with tears in his eyes. For him, it was hard to except that he is unable to be the part of a businessman's meeting. From the car window, BO was able to see that businessman few times and whenever he saw him, a drop of tear always fell near the window.

Lesson #3

When it's hard for you to accept ignorance from a person that matters the most to you, God will use that person to make you stronger and be prepared for a better tomorrow. You will become stronger and stronger every time that person will ignore you. Their ignorance will become your strength and your strength and will power will take you to a life you deserve.

When life has accepted you than no one's rejection should matter to you. This is what life should be, when your destination is clear than no obstacles should stop you or distract you from your desired goal.

For BO, the most important person was the businessman. He was able to see him few times from the car window and whenever he saw him, it became a lot easier for him to stay strong and have patience.

Finally, the businessman is coming! He looks a bit tired; I hope he is fine. BO said.

The businessman was tired from a day-long meeting. It was almost sunset when he came back in the parking lot. He tied up his seat belt and started the ride back to home. In between the ride he drank few more sips from BO and he was about to finish the last few sips from the bottle. By now BO was scared, he was thinking what if the businessman will throw him in the dustbin so soon. And this is what happened with BO!

After finishing the water, the businessman threw BO away from his car window to a dustbin. The dustbin was on the roadside near an old hand-pump on the highway. BO was shocked, for him this was something unimaginable. He never thought of this before in life, but it has something for BO and some lessons for us!

BO was on the corner of the road inside a dustbin shocked and nervous; he did not know what is going to happen next. Let's help him and give him some hope and energy to survive.

Hey BO! Are you feeling, ok? I asked.

Not really Aly, BO said sadly, I was expecting luxurious life and paparazzi but see where I am right now, a trash bin. BO added.

Listen BO, when life is not going as per your wish, it means life will give you something more valuable than paparazzi, I said.

Life, ya right! Why not, it sucks badly and more importantly, Life don't LIKE ME!!!! BO screamed in anger.

Ok hear me out, have you ever seen this beautiful sky full of fluffy clouds and clean like crystal before? I asked.

NO, and I would never have, if I were chilling in the fridge. BO added.

This is what life is giving you BO, this amazing view of life that is out of the fridge, the real world is way more different than you have imagined, I said.

Ya, really? A setting sun with some white clouds and the smell of trashhhh, BO said.

No no, you will get out of this situation soon, just have some patience, I added.

Please Aly, do not say these words, I am very hopeless now and.... never mind, said BO sadly.

And what BO, please share it with me, I insisted.

I want to give up and go back to the recycle centre, I cannot live like this, BO replied.

Please don't say these words, life is very precious and we only live once; Never lose hope BO, there is always something good at the end, I added.

Fine, just be with me; BO said.

We are always there with you BO! I said.

Time passed by and it was evening already, till then BO was feeling really hot and sweaty. It became harder for him to stay strong but he had to keep up with hope and patience.

BO, how are you? I asked.

Pretty ok, was just looking at the sky and hearing some car horns, BO replied.

Hey, can you see the beautiful sky with lots of shining stars and the gorgeous moon? I asked.

Yes, I can. It's beautiful, BO replied.

Have you seen this sky before? I asked.

Not in reality but yes in the television in the supermarket. I do not know how I am saying this, but I am grateful that I am able to see this beauty today. BO replied.

See, this is what I was telling you. Had you not been to this trash bin, how would you have enjoyed this beauty? Remember, everything that happens with us, happens for a reason. If you are here in this situation, there is something life is planning for you, I added.

Ya, but this smell is just badddd, BO said.

Ok, fine BO! just enjoy the moment and forget about the smell. I said with a smile.

Lesson #4

If life is putting you in situations that you had never thought of, there is something valuable coming for you. Because life always takes the test before giving us a rewarding prize.

When we first met BO in the supermarket, he was a little bit egoistic about who he was but now, he is grateful for what life did with him. Life is the best examiner and the best reward giver also, when BO was egoistic, life thought to take a test and teach him some valuable life lessons.

He was left behind in the trash for 2 long days and these days were harder for BO. In these two days, BO was having a close look of how life truly is and what the real outside world looks like. While lying in the trash, he suddenly fell down due to strong wind. This situation made BO even sadder. He looks at the clouds in the morning, listens some birds' song, he sleeps with the moon and the stars, and wakes up with birds and the sun. He was somehow trying to enjoy the decisive moment and show gratitude towards the situation but in reality, he was somewhere terrified too.

Then one day, a man came near the trash bin and looked at BO with an eye of satisfaction and ray of hope.

II

A New Life Begins

Hey Aly, someone is staring at me; BO said.

Yes, I know, you don't worry I am here; I added.

The man was a janitor in a warehouse and on the way to his work, he was looking for a bottle so that he could carry water to his work and then he found BO lying down near a trash bin all alone and scared.

I think he needs you BO! I spoke.

Really, does someone really need me? BO said.

Yes, finally you are going out of this trash bin, I said.

He picked up BO, he cleaned him with his cloth and then he took him to the handpump near the road side. He cleaned him with water and filled him to the top and took him to the factory. From here BO's new journey begins.... We are with you BO! don't worry. BO was feeling like he got a new life, a new beginning, and yes it was an amazing and new life for our dear BO.

Wooow, I am free from the trash bin and going somewhere; BO said while riding the bicycle with the janitor.

Yes, BO as I said; Have patience and everything will be alright. I spoke.

After being free from that trash bin, BO was finally feeling relaxed and happy. He was satisfied just by the fact that he is being used again, he was happier. But life had a surprise for BO. He didn't know that the warehouse, that janitor was working, is the businessman's factory who first brought BO from the supermarket. Yes, BO was somehow going to the place that belongs to his old friend. Let's see, what happens when they face each other?

Wow, this cycle ride is way better than that expensive car ride, BO smiled and spoke.

Lesson #5

When you have faced difficult situations and understood the real meaning of life, then you find happiness and satisfaction in small little things also.

BO was relaxed and chill on the bicycle ride not minding about the hot weather or bumpy road. He was just enjoying the vibes of his new life and he understood that materialistic things are good sometimes but the real success comes from satisfaction about your life and whatever you have now.

After half an hour of bicycle ride, they finally arrived in the warehouse. BO was looking at the warehouse shocked, because the warehouse was extremely big and looked giant. This warehouse belonged to a company that sells household products. In the warehouse, the workers use to pack the household products for distributors who supply to the stores.

The janitor parked the bicycle in the parking and took BO with him inside the warehouse. When he took him inside, BO's eyes were full with tears and happiness. He was overjoyed and filled with gratitude. He did not expect to go inside, he thought the last time that happened would repeat again but this time it changed.

Hey Aly, this man is taking me with him; I am going inside a warehouse for the first time. I cannot tell you, how happy I am now. BO said with Joy.

I am happy to hear that BO, go in and make some new friends. I spoke

Yes, Aly why not; BO said.

See, this is what happens when you understand the real meaning of life. You are able to find happiness in small things also! For BO, happiness meant paparazzi but now it's all about the feeling of warmth.

BO was enjoying the moment and he was continuously observing the workers out there. The janitor kept him with other bottles, which belonged to different workers. Let's see what conversation the bottles are having after seeing BO.

Hmm, new member in our group, hi; said one of the bottles.

Hi, I am BO; what is your name? BO asked.

Well, my name is Lila; I belong to a trolley operator named Madhav. With whom did you come? Lila asked.

I came with a janitor, said BO.

Ohh, that janitor Sabu. He is a very hard-working labour here. I am watching him for the last 4 weeks now.

4 WEEKS, you are with the trolley operator for the last 4 weeks now? Really! BO asked with shock.

Yes, it's common here, wait... hmm... see that big blue bottle there, he is coming here for the last 7 weeks. He has seen a lot of changes and will see more, I guess. Lila said.

BO was shocked, he was looking at some of the old or maybe oldest bottles there. For him, it was new to see old bottles being reused for weeks.

Hey Aly, see... so many old bottles being reused for weeks. Can you tell me why is that so? Why they have to reuse it for weeks? Why they cannot send them to recycle centre and buy some new ones for them? BO asked with curiosity.

Hmm, your question is nice BO. Hear me out, the people you are looking at are the ones who work for their needs and whatever they earn, their earnings always go towards fulfilling the needs of them and their respective families. They don't have enough money or time to buy new bottles and send the old ones to the recycle centre. By using old bottles, they fulfil their need for water or sometimes any other thing that can be carried out in a bottle. Understood BO? I replied.

Yes Aly, they work hard for their basic needs and they give us the opportunity to help them fulfil their basic needs. BO answered.

Nice BO you understood the fact pretty well, I am proud of you. I spoke

Lesson #6

When you get the opportunity to help and support, feel free to help and give your contribution to those who really need them. You are blessed when you are capable to help others and make their life easier.

BO was able to see and feel the real pain of people who work day and night for food, water, and a shelter to cover their head. BO was now completely free of ego and nervousness, but he was feeling blessed that he is one of the bottles who got the opportunity to help those who really need them.

Hey, meet our new bottle member aaaa.... I forgot your name Sorry; Lila said with confusion.

Ha ha, my name is BO! BO replied.

Ohh yes, hey bottles meet BO! He is our new bottle member; Lila introduced BO with other bottles.

All the other bottles replied to BO and said Hi. BO was feeling on the top of sky now, he was extremely happy to have some friends.

Hey, see that bottle! He is the bottle of the peon of this factory's boss, Lila said.

Ohh! Ahh, who is the boss of this factory? BO asked.

Ahh, see I only know that this factory has a boss; Lila said.

Ohh, I see. BO said.

In between the conversation with the bottles, BO realised that all of the bottles have come from a different background. And they all have different families and their stories.

One of the bottles named Milo came from a very poor family. He lives with a boy who works in the factory as a tea server, and he has to take care of her ill mother as well. Therefore, he works hard to earn meals to stay alive and serve his mother.

Another bottle named Lila comes from a family were their lives 8 family under one roof and only two of them are working day and night to bring food in the plates of their family members.

And our dear BO, who was just picked up today will go with a single father who lives with his daughter Sneha. Let's see what lessons they have about their families and how their friendship goes. Enjoy making friends BO!

Hi BO! I am Milo, said Milo with a smile on his face.

Ohh hi Milo, Nice to meet you. how are you? BO asked.

I am good BO, thanks for your concern, said Milo.

Hey, tell me about you. Where have you come from and who is your friend here? BO asked.

Well, I don't have much friends here, I just talk to Lila sometimes or if she is not here, I just sit alone near a window and see the world outside; Milo replied.

Hey Milo don't worry, from now onwards we three are going to be the best friends. BO said.

Thank you, BO! I am super grateful you said that, but its fine. Milo said.

So that's final from now, we three are the best friends ever. Our gang will rock and in future people will give examples of our true friendship; BO said with joy.

Ha ha, Oh BO! you are super cute and yes, we are true friends! Said Lila while laughing.

He he!! BO replied.

Then onwards, their friendship began, these three bottles were having some great times together. Happy Friendship Day BO! BO experienced something like this for the very first time. When BO was in supermarket, he was superior there, no one was really his friend. But here he is one of them, so he has some true friends.

Hey, by the way Milo, with whom do you come? BO asked.

Well, I come with Raju, one of the tea servers here; Milo replied.

Ohh, nice I love the smell of tea but never tested it; BO said.

Don't worry BO, you will taste it soon; Lila said with a suspicious tone.

Confused BO somehow managed to ask; Hey Lila, tell us about your family, where have you come from?

BO, don't worry, we are neighbours. Madhav and Sabu, they both live next doors, so probably we will see each other occasionally after work hours; Lila said.

Ok, but I want to know now, please tell me about your family, please; BO insisted.

Ok BO, I come from a family of 8 where they all live in a house of 2 rooms. There are 4 grandparents, 2 children and one couple who works day and night to serve food to their family. Lila replied.

Ohh, so how is life there? Are they happy with whatever they have? Ahh, just tell me more, I really want to know; BO said with excitement and curiosity.

Ha ha, they all know how to live with whatever they have. They all are very sweet and I sometimes get the opportunity to go with that lady Meetu, who works as a domestic help. By the way, Meetu is Madhav's wife and his big supporter. She deeply believes in Madhav's will power and capabilities, she knows one day Madhav will do something unimaginable. On the other hand, those two little sweet kids, they are way naughtier and cuter at the same time. They live with their grandparents at home; they are not old enough to go to school, so they stay at home while their parents go for work. I don't know but they all have something in common and that is the high level of satisfaction with their lives. They barely eat two meals a day but they are very satisfied with their life. They only know that they all are healthy and living together, that is what makes them special and kind hearted; Lila said.

WOW, they are really some sweet people Lila; BO replied.

Yes, BO and I am super grateful that I am the part of this amazing family; Lila said.

Lesson #7

If you know the importance and power of togetherness then everything becomes easy to handle and every hard situation seems nothing to fight with. Because situation is neutral, only thing that changes is our way of looking at it, when you will see any situation with an eye of new opportunities, it becomes easy to find the right path for that situation.

Hey Aly, did you listen to Lila; BO asked.

Yes BO, I listened to Lila and see what I have for you. **When you know the importance of togetherness and you have a strong will power towards life than every situation becomes a festival of smiles and satisfaction. I replied.**

Yes, ma'am got it!! BO replied with Joy.

The bottles were having some amazing conversations and BO was learning many new and valuable things. Time passed by and it was near the time of going back to home from work. When BO will reach home, he will get introduced to his new family.

Ohh, see the time it's almost time to go back to home; Milo said.

You are right Milo, and one more thing, BO will get a surprise soon today; Lila said while smiling.

A surprise!? BO said.

The time BO exclaimed this, Raju and Sabu were coming near the bottles and Raju was holding cattle that had tea in it. When they reached closer to the bottles, Sabu picked up BO and drank the last few sips of water from him and then Raju poured some tea inside BO.

WHATTTTTT!!!!!!!!!! Now I have to carry warm tea? BO Screamed.

Yes BO, Sabu don't know how to make tea, so every evening he takes home some tea with him so that he can drink it in the morning before coming to work. I told you BO you will receive some surprise Ha ha; said Lila and laughed.

Don't laugh Lila please!!!! BO said.

Ok BO! I will not; Lila replied.

Hey Aly, what's going on? Please tell me; BO asked.

BO, you are a nice and helpful bottle, you are getting an opportunity to help someone who really needs you. Listen, when you get the opportunity to help, never step back from helping and showing your gratitude. Always help the needy ones with full heart and affection. Ok? Aly told.

As you say Aly, but hey this tea tastes delicious; said BO.

Really, did you like it? I asked.

Yes, I am loving it. Hey Aly, what do you think about Lila? BO asked.

BO!! Is there something you want to tell me? I asked.

No Aly, I was just asking; BO said in a shy tone.

Ok, enjoy your ride to home with your best friend Lila; I said.

BO had an amazing first day and he made some good friends. They said good-bye to each other and started their journey to home. BO was somehow feeling excited to go home and more excitement was for Lila, overall, they are neighbours. This was something that BO never imagined, he was really enjoying that bumpy road ride and carrying warm tea with him and we can say his big motivation of doing it was of course, Lila. While BO and Lila were going together, Milo was on the other route because Milo lived near the factory so it was like 10 minutes' walk from factory to home.

Milo was a little shy and sad bottle; he did not know how to communicate confidently or casually and this was because he was seeing someone suffering for life and another for food. His owner Raju was the only one earning in his house and the only one living with her mother. His father passed away 3 years back due to which; he had to quit school and start working. One more thing happened with Raju that was unexpected and unpredictable. His mother was diagnosed with cancer 1.5 years back. She is completely on bed-ridden; she cannot even sit by herself. Things were hard for Raju, he has to do all the house chores, make food, feed her mother before going to work and when he comes home, he goes straight to bed without even having a single bite of food. Milo was there with Raju for last 1.4 months, he has seen Raju suffering and working hard every day. Milo always wished for Raju's good life and her mother's fast recovery.

BO reached home after half an hour cycle ride with Lila. They said final good-bye to each other and went home straight with their friends.

The moment BO entered his new home; he was amazed to see a one-bedroom home where a small daughter named Sneha was waiting for Sabu, her father. Sabu kept BO on the side table near the window and showered his love to his daughter after a long day of work.

Hi my little princess, how was your day; Sabu asked.

It was amazing daddy; I enjoyed my school a lot and I hope you also had an amazing day; Sneha said.

Yes beta, I had a great day. Come on let's cook dinner together; Sabu said.

Don't worry dad, I have already prepared some khichdi for us. Wait, let me do the plating. Meanwhile you change your clothes and get freshen up. I'll do the rest; Sneha said

BO was looking at this father-daughter bonding for the very first time. BO was continuously looking at them and smiling while having few tears in his eyes. BO was somehow feeling the emotions very deeply and was understanding what true love and affection looks like. BO was finally getting the view of the real world and the real true hearted people.

BO! what happened? You are crying. I asked.

Hey Aly, I am feeling something that I never felt before. I can feel love and see, the true bonding between this father-daughter; BO replied with wet eyes.

You are feeling the real emotions that run this world. You know BO, when you shower your blessings to the ones whose presence matters a lot for you, this universe makes your hard times easier and you become a better version of yourself. And, as you know, everything goes well at the end. I replied.

You are right Aly; this world is very beautiful and, as you told me, life is precious; BO said.

Lesson #8

Life gives us opportunity to shower our good vibes and blessings to those who give our life a motive to wake up every day. And when you feel these emotions deeply from your heart, eventually you get a better understanding of love & gratitude.

Life always tries to make us a good person and to do that, life gives us millions of opportunities. And the people who really grabbed those opportunities and accepted that they can change one's life for better cause, are the people whom we call great. Greatness comes from the way you treat your loved ones and the society you come from and not from having tons of cars in the garage and still you are unable to spread love and warmth.

BO was feeling relaxed and cozy there. And he was able to enjoy the sparky stars and moon with a smell of wet grass because that night it was raining and BO was really enjoying the rain and the cool wind.

Hey BO! How you feeling? I asked.

Hey Aly, I am feeling just awesome and see the weather, after the rain, is so cosy and comforting. Oooo, the cool wind just kissed me in the cheeks. BO said.

Nice BO, you are really enjoying your new life. I am seriously feeling great for you. I said with a smile.

Shhh, Sabu and Sneha are sleeping. Let's just don't disturb them, OK? BO asked.

Oh, yes of course! Good night, BO, enjoy your night; I said.

That night BO slept so peacefully and calmly like never before. He was enjoying the cosiness of night and love and warmth of Sabu and Sneha. On the other hand, Milo was tensed to see Raju that he didn't eat his dinner this time also and his mother was sleeping unconsciously. And our Lila was ready to go with Meetu the same day. Madhav is taking a holiday today so that he can spend some time with his kids and parents thus, Meetu will take Lila with her.

Ohh, I can see the first ray of sun; BO said.

Good morning, Aly; BO greeted.

Good morning, BO! did you sleep well the last night? I asked.

Yes, Aly I slept the best. Ahh the wind that was coming from the window was amazing. BO replied.

Really! I am so happy that you enjoyed and relaxed the last night; I replied.

Today will be different from yesterday for all three of them. They all are not going to the factory; they all are going in different directions. Lila will go with Meetu; Milo will stay with Raju's mother at home and Our BO will go to school with Sneha. Let's see what new they are going to experience today and what they will teach us.

Hey Aly, I think Sneha is taking me along instead of Sabu; BO said.

Ohh really BO! you will experience the school life for the first time; I said.

School life? But I want to meet Lila and Milo; BO said.

Come on BO! try to experience new things and see what different the world looks like; I insisted.

As you say Aly, but only this time. From tomorrow, I want to be with Lila and Milo; BO said.

Ok BO! enjoy your day; I greeted.

This time BO was containing glucose water. Sneha takes glucose water to school every Friday because on Fridays the school students go for outing in the nature. So, for BO it was kind of a first picnic and for Sneha a new water bottle.

On the other hand, Lila was off with Meetu for her domestic help's job. Meetu works with an engineer's family and she is working for them for the last 3 years.

While Milo, he was an empty bottle sitting on the table top near Raju's mother. Like this their day began and one thing for three of them, All the best three of you!!

Looking at the sun and clouds BO reached the school within 15 minutes of walk with Sneha. While entering the school, BO was a little nervous and a bit scared too. Let's cheer him up!

Hey BO! why so nervous? I asked.

Hey Aly, I don't know but I am scared. See there are lots of children here, what if I get lost in the crowd or what if they will throw me off? BO replied.

BO! relax! You are in safe hands, look at Sneha, she really cares about you and why would somebody throw you away? Huh! There is no point of throwing you away; I asked.

Aly, I was thrown away from an expensive car, remember? BO said.

BO, that was past and this is present and if we are talking about past, you were picked from that trash bin and you become a water container for a janitor and his daughter. You are a big helper for two of them BO; I said.

Lesson #9

Never let your bad memories from the past ruin your present. Learn from past but never let your past overpower your present and make it worse.

Present is meant for enjoyment not for worry for future or remembering some bad events that happened in the past. BO was scared because he was thrown once, but he forgot that he was picked and reused. We should learn from past memories where something went wrong in our life and we should cheer ourselves from some good past memories as well, so that we can enjoy what we have today. Being afraid is good but overpowering that emotion is not that appreciable. Life will take tests in every mile of your life, be a bit scared its good but never too much. Too much scared emotions block our mind from creative thinking and ruin our problem-solving skills.

From this lesson, BO was feeling a bit light but not fully. While Milo was looking at Raju's sick mother coughing and sneezing. He was feeling very bad for Raju but unable to help. He was usually spending time by looking outside the window or thinking about

Raju. Moreover, Lila was neutral. She was sitting at the counter top in the kitchen while Meetu was cooking some delicious food for the engineer's family. They all were having a good day but somewhere they all missing each other.

Hey Aly, I think Sneha and her classmates are going somewhere. BO asked.

Hmm, I think BO; they are going for a picnic spot to enjoy their lunchtime. I replied.

A pic...n... what? BO asked confused.

A picnic spot BO. It's a place where people go with friends or family and enjoy sometime amidst nature, they play games, they eat food, they enjoy together and return home; I answered.

Ohh, a place to enjoy and eat near more trees; BO said.

Yes, kind of! You will enjoy the time in the picnic spot. You will be surrounded with nature, birds, more people who loves nature and many more; I replied.

Ok then Let's Go for picnic; BO screamed in excitement.

BO, Sneha and her classmates were ready to go for a picnic in afternoon, but suddenly it started raining and they have to cancel their plans. BO got really sad and started to scold the nature.

HEY ALYYYYY, see this nature doesn't want me to go for picnic and see a lot more nature; BO screamed.

BO! relax and calm yourself. What will happen if you keep screaming and scolding this beautiful nature given by God; I said.

NATURE WILL LISTEN TO ME!!!!!!!!! It will stop raining and I.... wait what's that? Colures in clouds!!?? BO said.

While BO was expressing his anger and frustration, a big rainbow appeared in the clouds while raining. Everyone started to scream rainbow, see a rainbow!! Everyone gathered near the classroom's window and saw that beautiful rainbow between the clouds. BO never had seen a rainbow before so for him it was the first time.

Hey Aly, see a beautiful Rainow!! BO said.

It's beautiful but it's not a Rainow, it called Rainbow; I said.

Ohh! A rainbow, nice!!!! I have never seen this type of a thing before; BO said.

You see BO! everything happens for a reason. On a sunny day you won't get the opportunity to see a rainbow and you know what, rainbows are rare. They are never seen every time it rains, they are seen rarely when sun and rain both are together, a rainbow forms; I said.

Hmm, you are right Aly. Sorry for overreacting! BO said.

Hey BO! Don't worry, we are best friends and in friendship no sorry, no thank you; I said.

Lesson #10

If we have courage to face any difficult situation with confidence then there is something great on our way. And if we are able to grab that big opportunity, we will make the biggest change in our lives and the society we belong to.

BO! was deeply and fully enjoying the moment. He understood one of the biggest lessons that; everything happens for a reason. And yes, that is absolutely true, without any reason we are not breathing also. We all are born to accomplish something great in our lives and we are alive to make an impactful change in this society.

And you know what impactful change BO will bring in this society? He will become an inspiration for millions and he will add values to the people who want to achieve more in life!

Moment passed by, the rain was over and it was time to go back to home. BO was ready to go back and he very much enjoyed his very first day of school. On the other hand, Milo had a rough day, moments back Raju's mother got extremely sick. She was coughing and sneezing very badly, the neighbours heard her voice of being extremely sick and they called Raju immediately. When Raju arrived, he took her mother to the nearest hospital and Milo, he was holding some fresh warm water for Raju's mother on the way to hospital. Now, Milo was in the hospital with Raju and her mother. Milo was continuously standing near Raju's mother and was very upset from the situation of Raju and his mother. Soon the doctor checked his mother and said that she will be fine. This was the relief for Raju and Milo. We wish Raju and Milo best of luck!

BO returned home with Sneha and Lila. Yes, on the way back home Meetu saw Sneha and they decided to walk home together. And our dear BO! was extremely happy to see Lila.

Hi BO! Lila greeted.

Oh, Hi Lila! Nice to see you again! BO replied.

How was your day, BO? Asked Lila.

Ohh, my day was awesome. You know what, I went to school for the first time!! BO said.

Wow! Great BO, I have never visited a school before but I'd love to; said Lila.

You never visited school, why? BO asked.

Because the kids in my family are not old enough to go to school, that's why I have never visited school before; Lila replied.

Ohh, I see. But hey Lila you know what I saw today? BO said.

What BO? Lila asked.

A rainow! BO replied.

A what? Rainow?? Lila asked in confusion.

Yes, a rainow that comes when rain happens with some light of sun; BO replied.

Ohh! You mean a Rainbow, right? Lila asked.

Yes yes, a rainbow. Have you seen one before? BO asked.

Yes BO! I have seen many rainbows when I was with my old family; Lila said.

An old family? You don't belong to them from beginning? BO asked.

No BO, before living with Madhav and Meetu I was living with a retired man who lived alone in mountains. And you know BO, when you live in mountains you get to see rainbows many times; Lila replied.

Then how did you come here? BO asked.

Well, one day that retired man decided to visit the countryside. He packed me in his backpack and we arrived here. The next day, he drank the whole water and he left me in the tea stall. There I met Madhav who picked me from there and took me back to home; Lila replied.

Ohh, did you miss your mountain life? BO asked.

A lot BO! I love mountains but from my love towards mountains, I have one of my biggest dreams, to visit NYC once; said Lila.

NYC!!! It's my favourite place too! Where you heard about NYC? BO asked in excitement.

Hmm, the retired man was planning to visit NYC before he decided to visit this village. I was excited that I would go to NYC once but it didn't happen; said Lila in sad tonality.

Hey Lila, don't be sad. Dreams do come true, you don't worry; BO said.

Thanks BO, you are a very sweet bottle; said Lila while smiling.

BO! was excited from inside, he was somehow feeling the emotion of love and togetherness. And it's true also, when someone is alive it's natural to fall in love and experience the feeling of togetherness.

Lesson #11

The feeling of love and warmth expressed for someone who really matters to you is what keeps this universe alive! Love is the gift from God to us, it keeps human motivated towards life.

Love gives us hope and path towards life. When we feel demotivated, our loved ones support us, shower their blessings so that we can move ahead and achieve more in life.

BO! enjoyed this beautiful walk with Lila and after some time they arrived at the spot where they had to say bye for now.

Bye BO! Take care, hope we will see each other tomorrow as well; said Lila.

Yeah sure, Bye Lila, have a great evening; BO said.

Sure, you too! Lila replied.

They said bye to each other, our dear BO was overjoyed, and he was experiencing some feelings towards Lila.

Hey Aly, look Lila also loves NYC just like me; BO said in excitement.

Yes BO! I heard your conversation, you two have some similarities; I replied.

YES, WE DO! BO screamed

Hey Aly listen, I need your help. BO added.

Yes BO! tell me what I can do for you? I asked.

Can you please tell me how can I ask Lila to be my friend forever. BO replied.

Hmm, BO! well just be yourself and go ask her the way you like to and remember, be confident; I replied.

Ok, but can you tell me the meaning of being yourself. I am myself than what is be yourself? BO asked.

Well BO, when a person loves someone and wants to express his feelings, he tries to become what he is not. Hmm, in simple words, people try to change their originality and become the person they are not, just to impress and express their thought confidently; I replied.

But why it's bad to change? Is it not good to become nicer? BO asked.

I am not saying changes are bad, and especially good changes, but I am concerned about the cause of change. Why will somebody change just to impress other, huh? Tell me, why cannot people stay the way they are. And you know, in this world, originality and trust are very rare. People are losing their originality just to fit in the crowd, they don't even think of stepping out of the crowd and creating a new crowd. Loosing originality never helps, what helps is being the way you are and you will find yourself being loved and appreciated. I replied.

I understood Aly, I will be and I will remain the way I am and never change to impress others. But I will change to become a nice person just for me; BO replied.

Lesson #12

Do not let originality and trust become rare. Be who you are and never break someone's trust. It is hard to find trust and it is even harder to accept that someone mistrusted us.

BO was super excited for tomorrow and he was expecting that he will go with Sabu to the factory and Lila will be there too. He practiced the whole night about what he would say to Lila and how he would express his thoughts in front of her. But it's not that easy! But BO, didn't know that his tomorrow will come after one week of his patience. See, I told you, life will take test in every situation.

When BO was practicing for his tomorrow, suddenly it started to rain heavily. The weather became very windy, rainy and super cold. Sabu had to close the window and he put BO in the side table of his bed. At that time Sabu heard people shouting; TSUNAMI!!!! He ran and opened the window and it was true that the wind was really strong, it was raining heavily and the weather was destroying trees, houses etc.

Sabu and his daughter got scared and they were really tensed about what was happening outside. While on the other hand, BO was confused. He was thinking, would he be able to go and talk to Lila? Come on! Let's cheer him up!!!!

Hey BO! how you feeling right now? I asked.

Aly, what is happening outside? Tell me; BO asked curiously.

BO! a tsunami is heading towards this village. Tsunamis are very dangerous; it can destroy any village in no time. I spoke.

REALLY, are these that bad? BO asked.

Yes BO, you better stay safe and be inside; I said.

But what about tomorrow? I was supposed to be with Lila tomorrow. Now, what to do Aly? BO asked with sad tonality.

Hey BO, relax; life is more important than anything else. If you are healthy and alive you can express your thought anytime. Just be patient BO! We are with you, I said.

After he came to know about the situation, he became sadder. It was his first feeling of love and he was ready to express, but for some reasons, it got delayed. Let's see How BO will stay strong.

HEY ALY, listen; BO screamed.

What happened BO! are you ok? I asked.

They are saying an alert has been announced due to tsunami and no one will go outside until the alert is over; now how long I have to wait? BO replied.

BO! I am sorry for you but be patient. As I told you, tsunamis are dangerous. For now, the first priority is to stay safe; I said.

How will I meet Lila now? How will I express my thought? Why me always, just why? BO said while crying.

BO! First, it's not just you, it's the whole village that is going through this alert. And second Lila is going nowhere you will meet her after the alert is over. Just have faith BO, we are with you. I told.

It's always me, first I was thrown in trash, I was there for 2 long days, and one day when I found my best friend it became hard for me just to see her. And you are saying it's not you... BO said while crying heavily.

BO! whenever life gives you challenges to face, you become stronger for better future. A better life will come to you soon and you know what, perception about every situation changes by changing your point of view. See BO, you got the opportunity to see Tsunami in your life and feel the real problems faced by people who are deeply connected to the soil and feel what does it like when nature expresses its emotion. I spoke.

I don't want to see tsunami; I want to meet Lila. Please wish for her good health, I can't live without her; BO said sadly.

BO! got extremely sad and he was losing his patience. He was continuously looking at the window in the hope that tomorrow the tsunami will get over.

The next morning when he woke up, the weather was same as yesterday. No changes in the weather at all! Where BO was sad because of not meeting Lila; Sabu and Sneha were worried about the food. They had enough food for a day but thereafter, they will have to buy some grocery.

On the other hand, Milo was still in the hospital next to Raju's mother. Her conditions were improving but she needed some medical treatment and rest. To buy her medicines, Raju had to work but he was unable to do so due to Tsunami. He was running out of money and if he won't work, he will have to take her mother back in the middle of the treatment.

And Lila, she was kept under the leaking roof to collect water. Due to bad weather, Madhav's house was leaking from few spots and they had to place some containers to fill up water so that their home does not get too much wet.

These were their stories due to bad weather. They all were having bad times and they all have to be patient and pray for better tomorrow. This tsunami situation became the most learning times for all the three bottles; they all learned different lessons and values. Let us see what they perceived and what we have to learn from them.

Hey Aly, BO said.

Good morning, BO! Are you feeling, ok? I asked.

Hmm, not really. I feel bad for Sneha and Sabu, they are running out of food. BO replied.

Ohh BO, I can understand your feelings but we have to stay strong. See, Sabu and Sneha are very intelligent people, they know what to do and how to handle this situation. I replied.

Hmm... but in the middle of this tsunami thing? BO asked.

Yes BO! This tsunami will help them to discover their superpowers and the amount of confidence they have. And you don't worry, life will give you opportunity to help them. You don't have to worry now, just wait for the moment and contribute your good vibes. I replied.

Anytime Aly, I am always there to help them; BO said.

BO was feeling terrible! He was willing to help them but you know what; all persons have to live their part of life. If they are in trouble, it's their part of challenges, we cannot live on behalf of them but we can pray for their better tomorrow. And you know what, life takes tests and helps us to discover the best version of ourselves.

The tsunami was becoming stronger and they all were losing hope. For a while the tsunami became so strong that Sabu's home started shaking.

Dad... the house is shaking; Sneha said.

Don't worry beta, just hold me tightly; Sabu replied.

It's very scaring dad, the home is moving fast. This is the only thing we own; Sneha said.

Beta listen to me; I am with you. If this home will not remain the same, we will be still together and togetherness is the best blessing we have got from God; Sabu said.

Lesson #13

When we are together, we can fight any situation without getting afraid of it. Because any bad or unwanted situation is temporary, what remains permanent is togetherness.

In this unwanted situation Sneha was not alone, she has the power of his beloved father. She is in safe and secure hands; nothing can cause her harm as long as she is in her father's arms. Parents can face any situation but they will make sure their kids are in a safe and secure place.

The house continued to shake for 10 minutes. Sabu and Sneha were extremely scared and our BO was lying down in the ground. The condition of the house deteriorated, there were cracks on the wall, all the things fell down and the power supply was also out. It was completely dark in the house and the condition was horrible.

After 10 minutes when the house stopped shaking, Sabu stood up and lit a candle. When he saw the condition of the house, he was in shock for few minutes. He could not believe it's his home; the whole house was a mess. And the food fell all over in the ground, he had lost the last bite of the food and water. Only thing that remained the same was togetherness, they were safe and together.

Dad, we lost everything!? Sneha said while crying.

No beta we did not! We gathered the ability to fight with any difficult situation; Sabu replied while wiping off Sneha's tears.

But we lost all the food and the condition of the home is not good; Sneha replied.

We will buy food for ourselves and we will rebuild this home. You don't worry, Hmm? Sabu Said.

Sabu was a very brave and hard-working man. He believed in hard work and faith. His simple formula is; If something bad is happening, it is happening for a reason. For him this situation was something he and his daughter could learn from and we all know life is the best teacher. Sabu was mentally prepared for his house renovation but he had something in his mind. He will renovate his home on his own and he will teach his daughter some of the carpentry skill. Let us wish very good luck to both of them!!

This was what it happened with BO, Sabu and Sneha. This situation made them stronger and helped them to be prepared for the tomorrow.

Hey Aly; You forgot me? BO said.

No BO! we cannot forget you, you are special for us, I replied.

Hmm, I am feeling really dizzy! The shaking of the home was unimaginable; BO said.

I can understand BO! but don't worry everything will be alright! I replied.

I know Aly, I know; BO replied in a tired tone.

Hey Aly, I hope Lila is safe and secure as the shaking of the house was strong and powerful. BO added.

Don't worry BO she is fine; I said.

BO didn't know what happened with Lila. Lila suffered from an accident. When the house was shaking, a small cupboard fell on her and she got buried under the cupboard. It took little bit time to rescue her. She was rescued in a very bad situation; she was flattened and was barely standing. Meetu helped Lila to stand properly and after sometime, Lila was kept back in her position to collect water from the leaking roof.

We can feel how hard it is to suffer from an accident and quickly get back to work. Lila was feeling really tired and her eyes were barely opening. But it was important for her to help Meetu and her family from this terrifying situation. She has to give her best to stay strong and help the needed once.

Our dear Milo, he was still there in the hospital. Raju got an amazing news; her mother was improving. And the Raju somehow managed to pay the hospital bill. So, it was the happy time for Raju and Milo as they both were feeling relaxed.

Lesson #14

The situation will be same for everyone, the only thing changes is what this situation teaches us and what it gives us while going back.

The storm situation is same for them, the only thing changed is someone got the opportunity to relax and be happy with their loved ones. And for someone this situation is hard to deal with.

After sometime when the storm calmed down for few hours, an announcement was made near Sabu and Madhav's homes. The announcement was made to ensure the village people that they don't have to worry about food and water. Food and water would be provided by an NGO, which was helping people during the storm situation. People, who needed food and water, had to bring their own containers and take food from the stall.

Sneha, you heard the announcement! We don't have to worry for food and water, Sabu said in excitement.

Yes dad! I am super happy now; Sneha replied.

So, it was time for BO to work and carry some drinking water for the family.

BO! It's time for you to get back to work and help them to stay hydrated; I said.

Ok Aly, I am always ready to help and send my good vibes to people who need them the most; BO replied.

BO was ready to help them. The time came when the second announcement was made and it was time to go to the stall and get some food and water.

The stall was about half a kilometre away from Sabu's home. He had to walk there and get the food. The difficult part was it was still raining a little bit so, he had to take his umbrella along with 2 bowls and few bottles for containing food and water.

Ok Beta, you stay here I am coming from the stall; Sabu said.

Ok Dad you take care Dad and stay safe; Sneha greeted.

Sabu started walking with a ray of hope that he could feed his beloved daughter with some food. So that they could sleep with full stomach. And yes, BO was going every time with Sabu to collect some water.

On the way there, BO saw Madhav coming towards them and guess what, Lila was also coming with Madhav. Lila's condition was not that great, she was looking dirty and yes, she was still looking flattened. Let's see what happens when BO and Lila meet.

Lila, is that you? BO asked in shock.

Yes BO! it's me; Lila replied in a soft tonality.

Wait, what happened to you? Are you ok? BO asked.

Well BO, I am not ok! I am tired and want some quick rest but the work is endless; Lila replied.

Really Lila? It's that bad; BO asked with tears in his eyes.

Yes, BO the situation is worst for me. I am collecting water that is leaking from the rooftop. And the water is leaking 24X7 and due to shaking of home that happened today morning, one small cupboard fell on me and I was under it for 5 minutes; Lila replied while crying.

Lila, I am feeling really bad for you, I don't know what to say but you please take care and try to have some rest; BO said.

It's not possible BO! I have to work so that my family can sleep properly and drink water timely. I can't take rest, it's important for me to work and stay active, Lila replied.

Ohh Lila, why are you so gentle always, huh? BO asked.

I am always grateful BO! Remember, I told you Madhav was the one who gave me shelter once again. It is my responsibility to give back to him and do my best for that family who thought me that I could be reused again, Lila replied.

BO was continuously looking at Lila who was tired and weak. She wanted to take some rest but she was aware about her responsibilities.

Lesson #15

Sometimes responsibilities become bigger than our own self. When we know we have to give our 100% to help those whose appearance matters us the most, we do not care for our conditions. What we see are the tasks that are important to complete for them.

Lila was aware about her responsibilities. For her, the most important thing was to stay active and do the tasks that were assigned to her. While she is working, her family can sleep peacefully.

When Sabu and Madhav reached near the stall; they saw a long queue. They had to wait for 40 minutes for their term. Sabu collected some fresh food in the container and collected some drinking water in the bottles. But guess what was BO holding? Any guesses? Let's ask BO!

Hey BO! what have you got? I asked.

Really Aly, you are asking me this right now!? BO asked.

Well, Yes BO! I just wanted to know, I replied.

Fine! I am holding some fresh, cozy, warm TEA!!!! BO replied.

Really BO! Nice, you are not just holding Tea, you are holding a drink laced with emotions, I replied.

I know Aly, I also love Tea. I have forgot the taste of water now; BO replied.

Ohh BO stop being so dramatic, I replied.

While BO was holding some Tea, Lila was struggling in holding some water. Her condition was becoming worse every minute. Let's hope that she gets the best of life!

Sabu and Madhav reached home; on the way BO and Lila said bye to each other. When Sabu arrived, Sneha opened the door.

Sneha, I am back with some fresh warm food and water; Sabu said.

Wow dad, come on and let's get some plates to eat; Sneha said in excitement.

You wait Sneha, you sit here, let me get the plates for both of us; Sabu Said.

Sneha and Sabu were super happy to see food in their plates. They had lost hope of eating food today but as we know, if life takes the test, it makes sure that no one ever sleeps with empty stomach. Today the food tasted extremely delicious for them and why not, they had a very rough day. After eating their food, Sabu cleaned the dishes and helpeed Sneha while she was making bed for sleeping.

Dad, where we are supposed to sleep now? The floor seems dirty and full of mess; Sneha asked.

Don't worry my little princess, I will do something; Sabu said.

Sabu quickly cleaned one corner of the room where the mess was less. He then spread a sheet on the floor and placed two pillows.

Sneha, for today we can sleep here and by tomorrow we will clean all the mess and we will sleep in the bed once again. Is that Ok for you? Sabu asked.

Yes dad, it's fine; Sneha replied.

They both slept peacefully and most importantly, safely. They were safe in their home. The condition of the home was not that great but it was fine for two people who are pillars to each other. On the other hand, this time BO was kept on the other window near the entrance gate. And guess what, he was able to see Lila from there.

Hey Aly, Look Lila is sitting on that window; BO said.

Oh Yes BO! You are right, I can also see her. I replied.

But Aly, look at her, she looks so tired and upset. I really want to help her but I cannot; BO said.

Hey BO! Relax, everyone has to go through some very hard phases in their respective lives and when they overcome them with grace, they become the best version of their selves; I replied.

I know Aly but just look at her, she seems so helpless and weak; BO said.

She is facing some hard time BO, but soon she will be fine like before; I said.

Aly, should I start the conversation with her? BO asked.

You should try to, maybe she will feel better after a conversation with you; I replied.

Ok Aly, let me talk to her; BO said.

BO! Don't forget to tell her what feelings you have for her; I said.

Aly, you still remember that? BO replied in shy tonality.

Yes BO! how can I forget that you like her; I said.

Ok fine, let me start the conversation Aly; BO replied.

Ok, ok start the conversation!! Best of luck BO; I replied.

Thank you, Aly; BO replied.

Hey Lila, BO shouted.

Ohh BO! is that you? Lila asked.

Yes, Lila it's me! How are you? BO asked.

I am fine BO! Thanks for asking; Lila replied.

I can see that you are sitting on the window, you are not inside today; BO asked in curiosity.

No BO! Tonight, I got some time to relax and felt some night wind near this window; Lila replied.

I am so happy for you Lila; BO said.

Thanks a lot BO! I really think it was nice talking with you; Lila said.

Anytime Lila; BO replied.

Tonight, it was the best time for Lila, she had the whole night to relax. The reason was, the rooftop was not leaking anymore because the storm had stopped for few hours. Between these hours BO and Lila were enjoying this beautiful night with cold cozy blowing wind. They both had some special feelings for each other. They wanted to share it but we can understand how hard it becomes when we have to share some special feeling to the person whose presence is everything we need.

Hey Aly, what to do now? I want to share my feelings but I am nervous; BO asked.

Hey BO! don't worry, just say what you have for her and don't panic. Express your feelings calmly and sweetly; I answered.

I have a lot to say Aly, it's not just I like her but I love her personality. She is so brave and caring bottle. I want to go near her and cuddle her so that she can relax and feel what I have for her; BO said.

Oh BO! you are such a nice bottle. I know one day it will be the day you imagined. For now, say what you have for her; I replied.

Yes Aly, it's time to share what I have for her; BO said.

BO was having some really strong emotions for Lila. He had a lot to say but you know, it's not always what we want, rather it's what good for us. BO was about to express his feeling but he saw Lila was sleeping so unconsciously that she didn't even realise. It's already morning and she has to leave for work.

Aly, its already morning and Lila is sleeping. It's too late to share; BO said.

It's never too late BO, the right time always comes and when the time will come the whole universe will help you to express your thought; I replied.

I hope so Aly; BO replied.

Lesson #16

The right time will always come for you to express your feelings to those who really want to be with you. You just have to be patient and hold your feelings.

BO! was really looking forward to share his feelings but he has to wait for the time when everything will be in his favour and this universe will help him to express his thoughts. And it's true, the hard part about life is waiting, we have to wait for the moment when our dreams will come true. In between, the life prepares us

for the best and the worst parts of life.

After few minutes Sabu woke up and took BO from the window to his table. The morning was beautiful and mesmerizing but the danger of rainstorm was still on. We all know when the first ray of sun is about to come it is time to drink some warm tea and get ready for the day. It was Sabu's cleaning day; he had to clean all his home and get rid of the mess that was all over in his home. But the beauty of the morning ended as soon as cold storm started to blow really hard. Sabu quickly closed all the open windows and he lit the candle for some light in the house. While all these were happening, BO was feeling really sad and tired. He was deeply concerned about Lila, he wanted to be with her but it was not possible anymore. He was so tired and unhappy with the situation that he quickly went to sleep.

Meanwhile, when he was sleeping Sabu and Sneha started to clean and repair their home. On the other hand, Milo was extremely happy because the health of Raju's mother was improving really fast and after this storm alert gets over, she will be discharged from the hospital.

And Lila, what to say about her she is still in the same situation, but we can see, how brave she is. She never takes back her steps from helping her family, rather she is always ready to help and support her family. Lila, you are a true inspiration for us.

We all know what hard times all the bottles and their families have been through but what is important is; they are with their family and they are learning some of the most important lessons of life, everyone ought to know.

Hey Aly, Good Morning; BO! Greeted while yawning.

Good Noon BO; I replied.

Noon? It's already noon? How long did I sleep; BO asked.

It doesn't matter how long you slept. What matters is you are fresh and active now; I replied.

Ya right Aly, I really feel fresh; BO said.

That's great BO! I am super happy for you; I said.

Aly, look the house is so clean and free of the mess. Who did all these? BO asked.

Sabu and Sneha were working really hard from today morning to clean this house; I replied.

Ohh, Nice! They are some hardworking people; BO said.

Yes BO! they are; I replied.

Sabu and Sneha were working really hard to make this building a home once again. They cleaned the entire floor, reorganized all the belongings and they were waiting for the rainstorm to get over so that, they can fix the cracks on the walls and some broken furniture.

Dad, the home is looking much better; Sneha said.

Yes Sneha, we worked really hard today and especially you, my little princess. You were so hard working and passionate today. I have never seen you working so much; Sabu said.

Of course, Dad I had to work for you and for my dear home. I really love my home and as long as I remember, we both have been in this home since years. So, I had to work; Sneha replied.

My princess I am really proud of you today. May this whole universe shower all the positive vibes and blessings on you; Sabu said.

Thank you, dad. But, the work is not yet done. we have to fix this rooftop and broken furniture; Sneha said.

Don't worry beta, once the rainstorm is over, we will do it in no time; Sabu replied.

Ok dad. But for now, I am starving! Can we have something to eat; Sneha asked.

Yes of course! Let me go to the NGO's food stall and get some food for us; Sabu replied.

But it's raining outside, how will you manage? Sneha asked.

Don't worry for me Beta. You just arrange the plates, I will come in no time; Sabu replied.

Ok dad; Sneha greeted.

Sabu quickly took the containers and bottles (BO was also there) to grab some food and drinking water. It was raining so Sabu had to carry an umbrella also. It was not easy for him to carry all of these things at once, but it was necessary so he had to manage. He left the home and reached the stall in few minutes. After reaching the stall he saw that only one or two people were arrived by that time. So,

Sabu was lucky he didn't have to wait in a long line for food and water. There BO saw Meetu coming towards the stall to get some food and water. But Lila was not there with Meetu.

Hey Aly, look Meetu is coming here; BO said.

Yes BO! she is Meetu; I said.

But I can't see Lila with her; BO said.

She must be busy BO, don't worry; I replied.

Busy doing what? Is coming here and collecting water not her job? BO said in angry tone.

Relax BO! It is not always necessary that one have to do the same thing repeatedly. May be she must be doing something more important; I replied

More important!! Yaa right, collecting drinking water is not important but sitting under a leaking roof is important; BO said.

BO! She is doing an important job by collecting water from the leaking rooftop. Because of her, everyone in her family is sleeping peacefully. Neither the floor got wet nor someone in her family fell sick during these though days; I replied.

Whatever Aly, you will not understand how do I feel right now. Please leave me alone; BO said.

BO! was very angry and upset. He wanted to meet Lila, he wanted to feel her presence but it didn't happen today. BO was thinking that sitting under a leaking roof is easy and not an important job but he didn't know how much courage it takes to sit under a leaking roof all day and night to catch every single drop of water. Lila didn't even get one second of relaxation, she was continuously working hard but BO was thinking something else. Meanwhile, Sabu collected the food and water from the stall and started walking back to his home. On the way to home, the rainstorm started to catch its speed and the wind and the rain become more powerful. The weather became so bad that Sabu quickly started to run. It was not easy for him to run in this bad weather but he had no choice, he had to save himself from rain and keep the food safe as well. After few minutes of running and brisk walking, he reached home. Sneha opened the door for him.

Daddy! Are you ok? Come in fast; Sneha said.

I am fine, due to bad weather I had to run. But you don't worry, I brought you some food; Sabu replied while gasping.

Daddy, you should have waited at the stall for the weather to be normal. I was fine here; Sneha said.

My daughter is hungry and I would have waited there, NO beta. I know you are very hungry; you needed some food and water. I had to come for you; Sabu replied.

You know what dad; you are the best but sometimes you do over; Sneha said.

For you princess, I can go beyond my limits; Sabu said.

Ok we will talk later; you can scold me anytime, but for now can we please eat. Now I am starving; Sabu added.

Ok dad, let me bring some plates; Sneha said.

After that father-daughter conversation they both went to eat their food. While they were eating, the rainstorm started to hit their village strongly. The wind picked up again, but this time the rain changed its course and reached inside Sabu's house. Yes, because of the crack on Sabu's roof, water started coming inside the house. The house was leaking all over.

Aly, the house is leaking; BO said.

Yes BO, the cracks on the rooftop caused the house to leak; I replied.

Ohh, now what? Do I have to collect them? BO asked.

May be BO! but don't worry we are with you; I replied.

Meanwhile, Sabu got really tensed from the situation. He quickly stopped eating and began his search for different containers, bottles etc, so that he can collect water from the leaking rooftop. And guess what, BO was one of the bottles who got the job to collect water from the leaking roof.

Really! Do I have to? BO asked.

You should BO! it's your responsibility to work and help your family; I said.

Ya right! Collecting bottles of water and sitting here; BO said.

BO! why are you overreacting? You were not like this; I asked.

I am just tired from this situation now Aly, I really want to relax and enjoy my days; BO said.

BO, everyone loves to enjoy his days but difficult situations are part of our lives. It makes us strong for our future; I said.

Tell me one thing, if we all live once, why do we have to face bad days, why not good days always; BO asked.

Let me ask you a question; you know the taste of water but had you been to somewhere else, would you have tasted tea? I asked.

NO! And I would never have if I were staying somewhere else; BO replied.

Ya right, but this is life, when we know the taste of good, we should know the taste of bad as well. Let's say, we eat different types of food everyday and most of the time, we don't repeat the same food for days. If we cannot eat same thing daily how you are expecting life to give you the same taste daily; I replied.

Lesson #17

Good or Bad are parts of our life, we cannot escape from it but we can escape from negative mind and see the possibilities in any situation

For BO and his family, the situation was same from the last 3 days and he was extremely tired but he cannot escape from it rather, he can give his contribution to his family and support them in this difficult situation.

The rainstorm continued for the whole night and so did the leaking roof. BO had to collect water from the leaking roof for the whole night and due to this, he was unable to sleep or relax. Whenever he wanted to close his eyes, one drop of water would wake him up. It was not easy for him to stay awake for the whole night.

Aly, I want to sleep my whole body is stiff; BO said while yawning.

Hey BO, I can understand your feelings, but we cannot change the situation now. Be patient, we are with you; I replied.

Now I can feel Aly what Lila had gone through. She had to stay awake for day and night; BO said.

Yes BO, she is a hardworking and dedicated Bottle; I replied.

Hmm, you know what Aly, I thought collecting water from leaking roof is easy but now I know the pain behind it. My legs are also hurting; BO said.

This is what many people face BO! People think that the problems of the others are not difficult and people also think that their problems are the biggest in this world. But things change when they put themselves in other people's shoe, they get to know the real picture of it; I replied.

You are right Aly, I was wrong about Lila and her conditions. Now I know the real pain she has been facing for the last 3 days; BO replied,

Lesson #18

Everyone's difficulties are different; we should never judge people with their situations. We never know what they are hiding behind a happy face.

BO was assuming that Lila was doing some very easy job compared to him but, when BO entered in the shoes of Lila, he got the chance to feel and do what Lila faced. This changed the way of BO to look at any situation.

Time passed by; BO was collecting every single drop of water, leaking from the rooftop. He was struggling and his whole body was in pain and his eyes were full of sleep. After struggling all night, one ray of hope touched BO's cheeks. Yes, finally after 3 days of rainstorm it was time for some good and sunny days. The ray of sun also cuddled the cheeks of Sneha. The moment she saw the sun, she immediately waked his father up.

Daddy!! Look SUN!!!! Sneha screamed.

Oh yes beta finally the sun light have touched the ground; Sabu replied.

Yes. Wait, let me open the window and the door; Sneha said.

The moment Sneha opened the windows and the door, the whole room was shining bright from the sunlight. The sunlight was reaching each and every corner of the room. This means that the rainstorm alert was finally over and now, one can go out and work.

Look Dad, the whole room looks like it's made of Gold; Sneha said.

Ha ha, yes beta the whole home is shining; Sabu said.

Finally, we will get back to our old routine! I can go to school and you can go to work; Sneha said.

But first we have to fix our whole house and then we can start our days all over again; Sabu replied.

You are right dad; we have to repair this home first and the big thing is it helped us to stay safe in this disaster; Sneha said.

You are absolutely right my princess; Sabu said while hugging his beloved daughter.

It was a relief for all the villagers, they all were happy and, you know what, the whole village gathered and started dancing in the sunlight. The best days were finally taking route towards this amazing village.

Hey Aly, finally the rainstorm is over; BO said.

Yes BO! you did it! You faced these days with full bravery and confidence; I replied.

Thanks Aly, but we did it. If I would have been alone, I don't think that I would have survived for one day. You made me survive these days; BO said.

BO! I helped you to discover how powerful and brave bottle you are. And yes, I think we did it; I replied.

After that beautiful sunrise, everyone went to work like they used to. We saw the power of togetherness and a positive mindset. They all fought this disaster with hope and a positive mindset.

Hey Aly, I was thinking if Lila would be okay or not. She had faced some really bad times; BO said.

Don't worry BO! We know what she had gone through but she is a very brave bottle, I know she would be fine; I replied.

BO! was really looking forward to meet Lila. He was only thinking about her, whenever he closes his eyes, he can only see Lila's face and he could feel her vibes and warmth. He was experiencing the true feeling of love. Yes, BO was in love with Lila, he wanted to express his feelings to Lila but life had some other plans for both. Let's see when he gets the right time to express his feelings.

Meanwhile, Sabu and Sneha started to clean and repair their home. The home was less messy but had lots of cracks in the walls. It was not easy for them to fix the walls but they started working towards it and tried their best.

Dad how we will fix these cracks? Sneha asked.

Don't worry beta, there is nothing in this world that we both cannot do together. We will fix these cracks in no time, let me just arrange the equipment's and some POP; Sabu replied.

Ok daddy; Sneha replied.

Sabu quickly went to get the required equipments from his neighbour. One of his neighbours works in a cement company, that's why he could get the required equipment and POP from there.

Meanwhile, Meetu also grabbed her broom and mop and started cleaning her home. While Madhav went out to bring some required stuff that were necessary for his home and kitchen. And our dear Lila, she was sleeping peacefully in the sunlight. Yes, Meetu had put all the bottles outside her home so that the bottles can dry and she can also clean the home easily.

And coming back to Milo's condition, Raju's mother was discharged and she had successfully arrived home. And guess what she was fully healthy and fit both mentally and physically. Now she was self-sufficient and she was enjoying her better life. But our dear Milo, he was already thrown in the dustbin. While returning back from the hospital, Raju threw Milo in the dustbin because he was looking dirty and crushed.

Sabu was back with the required equipment's and it was time for them to start repairing their home. First, they covered all furniture with bed sheets or any other cloth and guess what, they had to put all the bottles and some other cartons / boxes outside their home that means BO was finally able to see Lila. While they started to repair the home, BO was free to talk to Lila. But at that moment Lila was sleeping.

Hey Aly, look Lila; BO said.

Yes BO, I can see how calming she is sleeping; I replied.

Yes, Aly I know, I really don't understand When will I get the time to tell her what I feel for her. Whenever I see her, either she is busy or she is sleeping or about to sleep; BO said.

Relax BO! The right time will come for sure; I replied.

BO was thinking that only he has something to tell her but he had no idea that Lila also likes him. Yes, Lila was also feeling something special for BO but they both don't get the right time to talk to each other. But, we know life will give them the right time and the right place to express their feelings and start life together.

While BO was looking at Lila, he heard some sound coming towards him. It was the sound of a small garbage collecting truck that was approaching towards their home. BO saw people taking out waste garbage and putting in front of their homes, so that the garbage truck can collect. While the truck was coming closer to them, BO got really scared because he and Lila was kept outside the home and what if, Sabu and Meetu don't come on time to take them inside, they will be sent to the recycle centre. This thought made BO even more scared and tensed.

Hey Aly, look a garbage truck, what if this truck takes us to the recycling centre. I haven't talked to Lila yet; we have to spend good times together. WHAT WILL HAPPEN IF ME AND LILA WILL GET SEPARATED?!!! BO screamed.

BO! Calm down!! relax; I replied.

I can't relax Aly, just can't. Look this truck is coming closer and closer and no one is coming to take me and Lila inside. Wait, Sabu he is here, he will take me inside but what about Lila, where is Meetu??? BO said.

BO was extremely scared, he thought Sabu will take him inside but he came out with more garbage to put outside. And Meetu, she also came out not to take Lila inside but to throw away more garbage. And the moment came in, the truck stopped in front of Sabu and Meetu's home. The truck blocked the way, and BO was no longer seeing Leela, but he could hear the sound of bottles that were getting loaded in the truck. Soon the truck driver came to Sabu's home and took BO and other bottles from there and thrown BO and other bottles at the back of the truck. There BO saw Lila who was stuck in between the bottles and the boxes. They both made eye contact with each other with tears in their eyes.

Lila you, ok? BO asked with tears in his eyes.

Its over BO! we are going to the recycle centre; Lila said while crying.

Lila, please don't cry. You are... BO said.

BO couldn't control his tears, he wanted to say Lila his feelings but they both had no words for each other. They both were continuously looking at each other and crying. And then...

I love you BO! I love you; Lila said.

BO smiled with tears in his eyes and said,

I love you too Lila, BO replied.

And they both looked at each other and laughed with joyful tears in their eyes. And the final moment came when the truck stopped at the centre and started to take out the garbage for recycling.

Bye BO! Good bye! I will miss you; Lila said.

BO looked at her, she was going far away from him. He cried but he finally said.

I LOVE YOU LILA !!! and I know we will meet again; BO screamed.

There they both separated their ways in hope of meeting again.

THE END

18 Lessons From Bo!

1. Nothing remains with us forever, if today we have something, tomorrow we will have something completely different from the last one.
2. What we see from inside is not always the reality of any situation, there is a big difference between reality and what is shown upfront. To know the reality of the situation, we have to step outside, we have to accept the truth completely, we have to see the things as it is and then, we have to change our thought process accordingly. When you accept any situation as it is, suddenly you will see yourself enjoying it.
3. When it's hard for you to accept ignorance from a person that matters the most to you, God will use that person to make you stronger and be prepared for a better tomorrow. You will become stronger and stronger every time that person will ignore you. Their ignorance will become your strength and your strength and will power will take you to a life you deserve.
4. If life is putting you in situations that you had never thought of, there is something valuable coming for you. Because life always takes the test before giving us a rewarding prize.
5. When you have faced difficult situations and understood the real meaning of life, then you find happiness and satisfaction in small little things also.
6. When you get the opportunity to help and support, feel free to help and give your contribution to those who really need them. You are blessed when you are capable to help others and make their life easier.
7. If you know the importance and power of togetherness then everything becomes easy to handle and every hard situation seems nothing to fight with. Because situation is neutral, only thing that changes is our way of looking at it, when you will see any situation with an eye of new opportunities, it becomes easy

to find the right path for that situation.

8. Life gives us opportunity to shower our good vibes and blessings to those who give our life a motive to wake up every day. And when you feel these emotions deeply from your heart, eventually you get a better understanding of love & gratitude.
9. Never let your bad memories from the past ruin your present. Learn from past but never let your past overpower your present and make it worse.
10. If we have courage to face any difficult situation with confidence then there is something great on our way. And if we are able to grab that big opportunity, we will make the biggest change in our lives and the society we belong to.
11. The feeling of love and warmth expressed for someone who really matters to you is what keeps this universe alive! Love is the gift from God to us, it keeps human motivated towards life.
12. Do not let originality and trust become rare. Be who you are and never break someone's trust. It is hard to find trust and it is even harder to accept that someone mistrusted us.
13. When we are together, we can fight any situation without getting afraid of it. Because any bad or unwanted situation is temporary, what remains permanent is togetherness.
14. The situation will be same for everyone, the only thing changes is what this situation teaches us and what it gives us while going back.
15. Sometimes responsibilities become bigger than our own self. When we know we have to give our 100% to help those whose appearance matters us the most, we do not care for our conditions. What we see are the tasks that are important to complete for them.
16. The right time will always come for you to express your feelings to those who really want to be with you. You just have to be patient and hold your feelings.
17. Good and bad are parts of our life, we cannot escape from it but we can escape from the negative mind and see the possibilities in any situation.

18. Everyone's difficulties are different; we should never judge people with their situations. We never know what they are hiding behind a happy face.

Printed by Libri Plureos GmbH in Hamburg,
Germany